# Professor Valentine

## A BDSM Valentine Romance

### Darlene Cunningham

# Contents

| | |
|---|---|
| Title Page | V |
| | VI |
| 1. The Professor | 1 |
| 2. The Student | 11 |
| 3. The Kiss | 20 |
| 4. Valentine's Day | 28 |
| 5. Diamonds & Pearls | 36 |
| 6. Valentine Sex | 43 |
| 7. Epilogue | 53 |
| 8. Excerpt from Are You Protected | 54 |
| Rate Your Experience! | 59 |
| About The Author | 60 |
| Coming Soon | 62 |

# *Professor Valentine*

## A BDSM Valentine Romance

Darlene Cunningham

This is a work of fiction. The names, characters, organizations, places, events, and incidents are either products of the author's imagination or are used fictitiously. Any resemblance to actual persons, living or dead, or actual events is purely coincidental.

© copyright 2024 by Darlene Cunningham

All rights reserved.

No part of this book may be reproduced, or stored in a retrieval system, or transmitted in any form or by any means, electronic, mechanical, photocopying, recording, or otherwise, without express written permission of the publisher.

Published by Darlene Cunningham

www.darlenecunningham.com

Amazon, the Amazon logo, and (publishing co) are trademarks of Amazon.com,Inc.,or it's affiliates.

ISBN:

Book Design by Shannon Bond

Edited by Darlene Cunningham

Printed in the United States of America

# The Professor

Professor Valentine sat at his desk grading the first exam of the semester. He had a bright group of students and he'd been excited to see if it translated into their coursework. Thomas had been a professor at Spelman for two years and at forty-two he'd been one of the youngest in the School of Medicine. He'd been proud of the achievement since discovering he could no longer perform surgeries. Shaking away those thoughts, he flipped to the next exam.

Brianna Jovi. She was at the top of his class, and he'd considered having her as a Teachers Aide for the semester but decided against it. Not because she couldn't handle it. She'd been more than capable. Thomas hadn't been sure he could control himself around her. Brianna had beautiful brown skin, plump breast that were a perfect handful and an ass that looked as if it was pillowy soft. Her hair had been in braids, with curly pieces that fell around them. If he had her around him constantly, it could potentially lead to a scandal. Freaking gorgeous.

He smiled to himself as he graded her exam. "Ninety-eight. Damn near perfect." He licked his lips as he flipped the paper and moved to the next exam.

• ❤ • ❤ • ❤ • ❤ • ❤ •

Later that evening at home, Thomas enjoyed a glass of Louis XVIII when his best friend and former colleague, Nicklous Spencer, phoned.

"Good evening Nick."

"Good evening Thomas. I haven't heard from you in a few weeks. How are things going? School? The students? You?"

"School is going really well. I'm enjoying it more and more each semester. Exams just started hence my absence. Apologies, my friend."

"No worries. I know how it is. Surgeries have been kicking my ass since you left. They still haven't found your replacement."

Thomas looked at the golden liquid contemplatively before taking a sip from his glass. He walked from his bar to the living area, taking a seat on the sofa.

"Why not? It's not like I can come back." A sadness engulfed him. He took another sip of the Cognac.

"I believe they think you can. It's not a disorder but a mental block. At least, that's what we all have collectively concluded. Your dad…"

"My dad doesn't want to see me as a disappointment, so he had to have a valid reason for what happened." Thomas let out a huff.

Sensing his friend's frustration, Nicklous changed the subject. "Enough of that and your father. Do you have any plans for Valentine's Day? It has been a while since either of us have been involved in a serious relationship. I don't know about you but I'm ready."

"A single middle-aged man who's career recently went to shit. No, not unless you're introducing me to someone or taking me out, I have no plans. The women I see every day are off limits." Thomas said thinking of Brianna.

There was a brief silence before he spoke. "Actually, I can. Take you out I mean. There's a new club that's opened and I've gotten an invitation."

Thomas bit his bottom lip at the thought of having a night out. He needed to release some of the pent-up sexual attraction he had for his student. He and Brianna could never happen, but a body double would do nicely. Thomas looked towards the closet that held his flogger, ties and various toys that he hadn't used in a few months.

"What's the name of the club?"

Chuckling, Nicklous responded. "Diamonds and Pearls. So, are you open to going?"

"Why not? It'd be good to get a night out. It's not just for people in love but also people who are looking for it. I believe it's something I need to get my mind off her." He let slip.

"Her?"

Thomas said nothing.

"Valentine, don't hold out on me. Who is she and why can't you pursue her?" Thomas smirked at the excitement in Nick's voice.

"Brianna Jovi. A student in my anatomy class. A sexy vixen that's completely off limits." Thomas squeezed and released himself, thinking about how his dick would feel between her ass cheeks. His thoughts drifted to his hands around her hair as he pounded her from behind. His dick could feel her. He squeezed it again.

"Valentine? You still there?"

Thomas became slightly embarrassed but shook it off. Nick didn't know what he was thinking. "Yeah, I'm still here. Valentine's night sounds like a good idea. I'll see you on the day."

The call ended and Thomas stood. He walked to his bedroom with his erect penis in his hand. If this was the only way to have Brianna, he'd take it.

Thomas ran his fingers across the gold-plated sign on the door. It read, Dr. Alan Valentine, Chief of Staff. He took a breath and lightly knocked on the door.

"Come in." Thomas's dad answered from the other side of the door.

Thomas walked in as his father stood with a smile on his face. Alan rounded his desk and the men embraced each other.

"Good afternoon son. It's good to see you. How are things?" Dr. Valentine ask as the men sat opposite each other.

"Things are going really well dad. School is in full swing, and I have an elite group of future doctors this year."

His father sat back in his chair, tossing the paper he'd been looking over back on his desk. "Any general surgeons in the bunch?"

"A few of them show potential, but we both understand that minds often change during residency."

Dr. Valentine chuckled. "You're right about that." A brief lull in the conversation had his dad looking over, studying him. It was a tactic his dad used to gage if he should proceed with a difficult subject or if he should keep it light.

Thomas sat waiting for his dad to ask what he always asked lately during their interactions. He didn't mind, understanding his dad always came from a place of love and wanting the best for him.

Before his dad said something that would cause a disagreement, he spoke. "No, I haven't changed my mind about coming back to see if the tremors have resolved itself. At least not until I can figure out what's causing it." His dad took an audible breath.

"Dad, I agree. I want us to be that father and son duo we've always talked about, but this." He held up his hands. "Can't be forced until I figure out why this happened." He pointed to his head. "Up here."

His father held a tight lip smile with shining eyes. "Whatever you need from me, I'm here."

"I know dad." Dr. Valentine stood and walked to his son. He leaned down to him, kissing the top of his head. "Whatever you need."

•♥•♥•♥•♥•♥•

The students were not at their best this morning. Lethargy is the word that came to mind as they entered and took their seats. He'd experienced it himself as a med student. It was the reality setting in. When the lack of a personal life and hefty workload collided. They were juggling a social life, studying for exams, and cultivating personal and professional relationships.

Once everyone settled, he took time to make eye contact with a few and smile at others as he passed out a quiz. The audible groans and minor complaints made its way around the room. He continued going down the row, handing the first student a stack of quizzes to pass back.

Walking to the back to retrieve the extra quizzes, Thomas stopped in front of Brianna Jovi's desk. She was at the end of the row. He could barely contain his growing penis when she smiled up at him. Brianna had on a pair of joggers, fluffy boots and a long-sleeved Henley. The braids cascaded down her back and she had small baby hairs in a curly Q along the front and sides.

Thomas' dominance emerged, standing over her, bearing down at her perfectly sculpted body. He whispered, "Fucking breathtaking".

After a few more moments of admiring her, he reached for the papers in her outstretched hand.

"Good luck."

"Thanks Dr. Valentine."

"Professor Valentine is fine."

Brianna blushed. "My apologies. Professor Valentine."

Thomas turned and walked away to collect the remaining extra quizzes when all he wanted to do was open her mouth wider and insert his penis. He was so glad he'd be able to get a release at Diamonds and Pearls.

Back at his desk, he informed the students they had twenty minutes. "The goal is not to complete the quiz. The goal is to get all the ones you complete correct. A patient wants a proper procedure, not a rushed one."

Thomas sat and began grading papers of his own, occasionally looking up at the class to ensure no one was cheating or needed any help. His eyes settled on Brianna. She sat with her forehead wrinkled, biting on her bottom lip while twirling one of the loose curls falling along her braid. His dick was fully erect, but it didn't bother him. He was a Dom and doling out punishment or pleasure with a hard dick was something he was used to. Thomas could push the emotion aside. He imagined what type of person Brianna would be in the lifestyle. She definitely wasn't a Dom. Maybe service? Since she wanted to go into the medical profession but he wasn't picking up helper vibes. She definitely wasn't a slave, too eager to answer questions as opposed to waiting to be told what to do.

Thomas continued to watch as pre cum escaped the head of his cock. He watched her pout and frown. As if a lightbulb turned on, it hit him. She was a brat. Brianna looked up at him, frowned again, then looked back down. She had a question but didn't want to be disruptive.

Thomas squeezed his dick into submission as best he could before standing and walking back to Brianna. He stood behind her, leaned close to her ear, and whispered. "Did you have a question, Ms. Jovi?" It was the closest Thomas had ever gotten to a student. He inhaled the aroma of coconut and strawberries. It created more pre-cum in his boxer briefs. He took a ragged breath which caused one of the loose strands to move. Brianna turned slightly to him and her frown deepened. He didn't care if it was because she was uncomfortable. A good little brat had to submit.

Brianna huffed a breath that tickled Thomas's mouth and nose. She was chewing on Red Hot gum. He immediately wanted to bend her over and spank her ass for chewing gum in his classroom. His eyes traveled from her pouty, glossed mouth to her nose, finally landing on her eyes and that damn frown. She didn't speak, just huffed again. His cock was so hard it could probably smash the desk into pieces.

"Yes, Ms. Jovi?"

She met his eyes, seemingly unbothered by their closeness. She bit her lips and the grip he had on the back of her chair tightened.

Whispering, "Well Dr. Valentine, the cardiovascular system has many functions, not just one."

"Very good Ms. Jovi. And it's Professor."

She blew out another breath as Thomas' gripped tightened even more. If he didn't disengage soon, he would surely break the desk. Brianna shook her head.

"I know, but Dr. sounds better." He was right, she was a brat and if she was his she'd be tied up and flogged for the defiance.

"Anyway." He focused back on her. "If I discuss the many functions of the cardiovascular system, which by the way is the first question." She gave him a chastising look. "It will take the entire twenty minutes to complete." She frowned on a huff.

Thomas slowly removed his hand from the back of her chair, lightly gliding his fingers across her back, sweeping her braids as he did so, before coming to a full stand.

"Very good Ms. Jovi. So stop worrying about finishing all the questions and focus on what's most important." He walked away without looking back, but he could hear her huff and mumble 'smart ass'. His steps faltered. Thomas wished he would one day be able to punish her for that. "Definitely a brat."

# The Student

Brianna dropped her bag on the floor as she entered her apartment. She walked to the bedroom, collapsed on her back in the bed and sighed. Valentine's Day was this Wednesday and she had no date, no prospects, and no life. School would be her life for the next few years. Brianna understood that going in, but she didn't anticipate the lack of companionship being so difficult. She hadn't been in a relationship for a while, however she had encounters occasionally. Lately, the last six months to be exact, a man hadn't even breathed on her. Until today.

She smiled at the way Professor Valentine's breath licked her skin and how his fingers lightly ghosted across her back. She could barely continue with the quiz. Her ringing phone took her from her thoughts. Blowing out a breath, Brianna got into an upright position as she answered her phone.

"Hi mommie!"

"Hi baby! I was calling to find out how things were going with school. Your dad keeps asking. I told him to allow you time to get settled, but he wasn't having it."

Brianna laughed. Her dad owned his own practice and had been excited when she told him she wanted to become an obstetrician. Tears in his eyes, he hugged her tight. She smiled sheepishly as she remembered the conversation.

*"We're going to be a family practice?"*

*"Yes dad. A family practice."*

"Things are going really well. My anatomy class is one of my favorites, but it's pretty tough."

"If you need a tutor or any additional help, let us know and we'll do what we can on our end. I know your dad would video chat with you to explain anything you need."

As her mom spoke, Brianna thought of how he'd take her to work, explain anatomy, later quizzing her, had been the most exciting time in her childhood. She and her parents were close, but her dad, Dr. Jovi, had been her idol.

"Daddy at work?"

"Yes. He had a breech and had to perform a C section. I'll tell him I spoke with you and you're doing well."

"Thanks mommie. Do you all have anything special planned for Valentine's Day?"

As Brianna's mom rattled on about how her dad had planned the night, detailing all the activities, she felt lonely. She wanted what her parents had. They met and fell in love in college. It seemed as if the loved didn't diminish. They were each other's person. Brianna hadn't found or think she would find hers.

Undergrad, she spent most of her time studying and focusing on maintaining a high GPA in order to get accepted into the best medical program. Boyfriends and dating weren't on the agenda until him. Shane had a lot to do with why she engaged in rare hookups when she did meet a guy. Blowing out a breath she expelled those memories of Shane from her mind.

Brianna was a private person and didn't want to develop a reputation around campus. Men tended to prejudge her proclivities in the bedroom. Now she was in a new city, at a new university, and she had yet to get the release she needed sexually and emotionally. Men asked her out, but she had to be selective. She didn't want a man who wasn't a part of the lifestyle. As a brat, she needed a man that fully understood how to handle her, inside and outside of the bedroom. It'd been a long time since she'd had sex, even longer since she'd been in a relationship. Lately she longed for them both. All the Valentine's Day flyers around campus didn't help.

"Honey? Are you still there?"

"Sorry mommie. Yes, I'm here. It sounds like you and dad are going to have a fantastic time! I'm really excited for you."

"What about you honey? Any plans?"

"Yes!" she said sarcastically. "Professor Valentine and his anatomy homework are going to guarantee a lit night!"

Her mother sighed. "Oh sweetheart. You should go out and have some fun. Sunni is close by. See if you two can do the single Valentine's thing."

Just as Brianna was about to respond. Her best friend Sunni called. "Speaking of the devil. She's calling now. Gotta go. Love you mom!"

"You two go out, have fun."

"We will. Love you mom. Tell dad I love and miss him." Brianna ended the call.

· ♥ · ♥ · ♥ · ♥ · ♥ ·

"Bestie Bitch!"

Sunni screamed over the video call. Sunni was a vibrant, positive person who radiated light wherever she went. She and Brianna had met freshman year and became fast friends. She had been reluctant to tell Sunni about her sexual interest, even though they were friends. Not everyone approved. Not Sunni. She supported Brianna and wanted to attend some events with her.

"Brianna? What's wrong?" Sunni noticed her pinched brow and sadness.

"Aren't you tired of singledom? I mean, not really being single but just not having someone you can be close to, cuddle and be friends with? You know not a fuck buddy, but a friend? You fuck? And do other stuff with? Ugh, I don't know. Ignore me. It's just Valentine's blues."

Sunni poked out her lip while giving sad eyes. "Ah boo. You've been working so hard for the last few years. You have to take time to relax, refresh, and regroup."

Her expression quickly changed into a huge smile. "And I've got just the thing for us!"

Eyebrows raised, Brianna asked. "Us? What do you have in mind? I don't munch."

Both women howled in laughter. "Shut up silly!"

"I found a local BDSM club and paid an arm and a leg for tickets for Valentine's night."

Brianna took a serious look at her friend. "Where did you get this arm and leg from?"

"Okay, okay. Maybe my client offered me the tickets as a thank you for saving her event. She and her husband are in the lifestyle and offered the tickets as a thank you."

Sunni was a chef who catered private parties for the wealthy. Hence where her curiosity about BDSM came from. Some of those parties were "play parties". She had to serve food and drinks like people weren't getting sucked and fucked around her.

"You wouldn't lie to your bestie, would you? If so, it's a cruel joke. If not, I may become a munch for you."

"Shut up fool. My cooter is for men to munch on. Respectfully."

The women giggled.

"So how's Mr. Fine ass Anatomy professor?"

Blushing as she licked her lips, Brianna closed her eyes before speaking. "Hmm. Hair still a dark, thick and brown. His eyes still a piercing golden hue. Body lean and strong and the six foot four-inch frame is still looking lick-able." She opened her eyes and continued. "He was explaining something to me in class as his goatee covered face hovered near mine. His breath showered my face with the sweet scent of peppermint escaping his lips. His touch gave me chills."

"Bitch! He touched you? Where?"

"Just my back. I don't even think he meant to, but my pussy didn't care. She wept at his touch."

The women laughed together, then sighed simultaneously.

The conversation transitioned to school, work then life in general before they ended the call.

Brianna got up to shower, make dinner and study before going to bed. As she sat at her desk going over her assignments, and outlining notes for upcoming papers, she started doubting her abilities to really become a doctor.

What made her so special that she'd be able to offer women at such a delicate time in their lives the support and care they needed? And to give it to them successfully. Brianna didn't doubt herself often, but this semester had been difficult. The weight of the coursework, the lack of a relationship in addition to missing her parents left her defeated.

Brianna wanted a meaningful relationship with someone who understood who she was as a future doctor, a brat in the BDSM community, and a partner. She wasn't a monolith, and she needed someone who really got that and didn't judge the other parts of who she was. When men she dated found out about her sexual interests, they thought she was a sex addict. She'd disappoint them when they realized she wasn't on her knees twenty-two of a twenty-four-hour day sucking dick. Hence why she was boyfriend-less and was spending the most romantic holiday of the year with her best friend.

The next day, Brianna raced to Professor Valentine's office. He was strict about office hours and would lock his door leaving exactly one minute later. She raced up the stairs two at a time, her braids swinging wildly back and forth. She thanked the Universe she had worn her lime green Atoms, which were paired with joggers and a lime green sweater. Brianna had two minutes to spare when she rush through his door bumping into a classmate. She held out her hand, steadying the guy while apologizing.

She blew out a breath, fanning herself with her sweater. Brianna looked at Professor Valentine.

"Am I too late? To speak with you, about my paper?"

Professor Valentine gave the student she bumped into, permission to leave. He cleared his throat seemingly annoyed, which was a new one toward Brianna. He addressed her.

"I see you are the kind of person who believes that you should get my full attention regardless of who's in the room and whom I'm conversing with."

Brianna pouted. She didn't mean to interrupt them, but she needed to ask him about her paper. He was the one who ended the meeting with the guy, not her, so technically, it wasn't her fault. She tried to convey that message by placing her hand on her hip and lifting a brow with her mouth in a full-on pout. Huffing, "I apologize professor, however, I've been trying to get to your office hours for the last three days. My last class ends when your office hours do so…"

"My office hours aren't conducive to your schedule so you decide that interrupting while I was speaking to a student." Brianna attempted to interrupt, but quickly closed her mouth when he raised a brow. "Instead of knocking and waiting to be granted entrance, you decide it'd be a good idea to barge in?" Brianna's pout turned into nervous lip biting. "If you'd knocked and waited, I promise you I would've given you all the time you needed Ms. Jovi."

Brianna's stance became a little less defensive. His piercing eyes scolded her as she removed her hand from her hip, straightened her brow while not losing eye contact as she looked at him, now through lowered lashes. "Thank you, Ms. Jovi. You can come closer and we can discuss your concerns." Once she stepped to his desk, he stood. Peering down at her, he raised his finger to her lip, pulling it in a downward motion. Brianna removed her lip from between her teeth and waited.

"Thank you Sir and I apologize for barging in. It's just..." Professor Valentine lifted his finger and Brianna again closed her mouth. "If you justify your rudeness with an excuse, it's not a genuine apology, is it?" Brianna notice the small smirk as if he gained satisfaction from chastising her. She had to admit, it turned her on.

She approached Valentine with butterflies fluttering in her belly. Brianna didn't know if it was fear or excitement however, she welcomed the mood. She bowed her head again. "My apologies sir, and you're right."

Thirty minutes later, Brianna exited Professor Valentine's office overheated and turned the fuck on. "What the fuck was that?" She questioned, walking across the yard to her next class with wetness pooling in her joggers.

# The Kiss

Thomas had been distracted all day after meeting with Ms. Jovi. The way she stormed into his office, flushed from running with perspiration gathered at her nose had his dick throbbing. His Dom had been itching to come out, especially when she sassed him and pursed her hand on her hips with that attitude. She's definitely a brat. A brat that needed correction.

The outfit she had on said she wanted to be noticed, and he noticed. The lime green sneakers with the mohair lime green sweater against her beautiful, smoky brown tone had her skin glowing. Her braids were falling down her shoulder and he longed to wrap his hand around them, tugging her head back to lick the sweat he knew was along her collarbone. He didn't notice her ass until she turned to leave. He could tell she didn't have on any underwear the way her it moved as she walked. God, he wanted her.

Classes had ended, and he considered indulging before the Valentine's event. Brianna's brattiness had him eager to play. He was a Dom and Dom's were patient, but could he wait until Wednesday? It would be difficult. Brianna stirred things in him he hadn't felt in a long time.

Shouting jolted Thomas out of his thoughts. He heard arguing in the parking lot that got louder and louder the closer he got to his car. He hurriedly walked toward the raised voices, noting one of them was a woman. A woman in distress. As he got closer, he saw Brianna with her finger pointed at some guy who'd had his hand wrapped around her arm. Too tightly. Thomas growled.

The man had been dressed in scrubs, with a stethoscope around his neck. He had strawberry blonde hair, a clean-shaven face, and stood at about six four. His height had been much taller than Brianna's five foot four-inch frame. Thomas's his heart rate pick up the closer he got realizing she was in tears. He approached quickly but calmly, placing his hand over the young man's which was still wrapped around Brianna's arm. He took his other hand and pried it away from her person.

"I'm Professor Valentine." He address the man as he freed Brianna's arm. The man released her and looked at Thomas.

"Is everything okay here?" He looked from the guy to Brianna. She remained quiet but Blondie tried to assert his dominance by holding his head higher and standing taller

"Good afternoon Professor. I'm Shane and I was just having a word with my uh-"

"Ex!" Brianna said loudly.

Thomas released her arm, turning to face Shane. He and Brianna were having more than a word. At the least it was a minor disagreement, the most an impending fight. Thomas experienced a myriad of emotions in the short time he'd arrived. Anger at seeing someone with their hands on Brianna aggressively but also compassion when he saw the tears in her eyes. And then relief knowing Shane was an ex. He also got joy knowing she was open to dating outside of her race. He closed his eyes, took a breath and addressed Shane.

"It looked like more than a disagreement, Shane."

"Exactly, I didn't and don't want him touching me." She sneered at Shane as she wiped the tears from her face. Brianna was trying to hold it together, the sadness and tears trailing down her cheek had Thomas wanting to break Shane's neck. Brianna rubbed her arm where a bruise had bloomed.

"Look, she's being unreasonable. Professor." Shane addressed Thomas. "Have you ever made a mistake you've regretted? Tried to make amends, only to have the woman you love dismiss it and treat you like leftovers?" The entire time Shane's eyed Brianna with his jaw slightly ticking as if he was holding back anger. Thomas didn't like it.

"If I'd made a mistake, I wouldn't have grabbed the arm of the person I'm apologizing to as aggressively as you had hers moments ago. It may be best if you go cool off and try to call her later."

"Yeah and not pop up on campus, surprising me with this bullshit. Better yet, don't even call. I told you a year ago, six months ago and now." She stuck her index finger back in his direction.

"Brianna? Be reasonable. I've apologized. What else do you want from me?"

Thomas spoke. "It sounds like she wants you to leave her alone. For good." He got into a staring match with Thomas but backed down when he recognized Thomas was just as dominant as he was. He turned to Brianna. "You're being very bratty right now and I'm not pleased. Actually," Shane said with his eyes focused on hers, "I'm disappointed in you baby girl."

Thomas had to contain his rage when he saw Brianna react by softening her stance like a good submissive. Only it was to the wrong dominant. Shane was no longer hers, but when a submissive, a lonely submissive needed a Dominant, they often submitted to any Dominant, which wasn't good.

"Brianna? It's time for our meeting regarding you assisting me in the classroom this semester. Are you ready?" He didn't wait for her to respond. Thomas caught her bag that had begun a slow descend down her shoulder, turned her towards the building and walked them away from the ex.

"Brianna!" Shane yelled. She turned to him. "Remember what we are." She nodded with her head down as she continued to walk.

Thomas was seething. He couldn't believe a Dominant would use his power over a submissive to control her unethically. He wanted to go back and confront him, but how? He was her professor not her protector, her Dom. Thomas couldn't do anything unless and until Brianna agreed to it.

Back in his office, Professor Valentine handed Brianna a bottled water as she sat on his couch biting her lip with her head bowed and eyes down. She was still submitting to Shane even though he wasn't anywhere near her. She's yearning for a Dom, yearning for someone to submit to. Yearning for someone to put her first so she could focus on other things. How had he not recognized she was flailing? Not only did she need a Dom, she wanted one.

"Brianna!" She popped her head up in his direction.

"Yes, Sir?" Her voice was low. So low. Thomas understood the risk, but he couldn't allow her to remain in this holding pattern.

"You are no longer dating him?" She shook her head from side to side.

"Use your words. I need words." Hope sparked in her eyes at the words most Dom's used when asking for consent.

"No. We broke up over a year ago. But he has this hold on me and won't let me go. Not fully."

Thomas walked over to her, sitting down, he took her face in his hands. "Snap out of it Jovi. Snap out of it." Thomas said forcefully.

"You no longer belong to him." He held his face so close to hers their noses practically touched. He couldn't resist, he took her lips, took control of her tongue, the kiss and her body. Thomas gripped her face harder as he continued the kiss. She didn't resist. Leaning into him, it's as if she craved it.

Once he released her mouth and face, he searched her eyes. "I apologize. That was inappropriate. But it seemed as if you needed… something." She seemed calmer. He waited. She leaned in closer to him, asking for permission with her eyes. He nodded. She took his mouth, slipping her tongue in. It took every ounce of strength not to touch her anywhere else or with anything other than his mouth.

After their tongues explored each other's mouths a few more moments, Brianna ended the kiss. "Thank you." She reached for her bag and stood. "I think Shane's under stress. He's completing his residency and is probably thinking he has no control over things. And when that happens, he needs to control something, well someone, in return." She looked down and whispered, "It use to be me."

Brianna walked toward the door as he stood. "I apologize for kissing you. That was unprofessional as your professor. I just, I didn't, I'm sorry."

She blushed. "Don't apologize. It helped more than you'd know." She turned and walked out, closing the door softly.

Thomas plopped on the chair and blew out a large breath. He was momentarily overwhelmed by everything that'd transpired in a little over thirty minutes. He found out she dated interracially and was in the lifestyle. Brianna was very receptive and didn't shy away from him. She embraced it. His dick stretched in his pants.

Thomas entered the hospital heading toward his dad's office when he saw his friend Nicklous walking towards him.

"Nicklous."

"Hey Thomas. Are you here to meet with your dad?"

"Yeah, we're going to have dinner tonight. Mom's having a girls' night and dad wanted to get some quality time with his favorite son."

"What are you talking about? You're not just his only son, you're his only kid." They both chuckled.

"So, Are you ready for Wednesday night? I have to admit I'm excited. I think I'm going to meet my person."

Thomas eyed Nick skeptically. "Your person? As in your soulmate?" He playfully pushed his friend. "Get the fuck outta here." He scoffed.

"Why? Because it's a sex club?" He whispered as he looked around. "I can't find my one? So women who frequent a place like that aren't worthy of a relationship?"

"No, I'm not saying that at all. It's hard to find your one but to find her in a club, any club is hard to believe. However, if you think you'll find her there, then so do I."

He embraced Nicklous patting him on the back.

"Honestly, I hope mine is there as well."

His dad walked down the hall. "Will you two stop making out in my hospital? Nick, let go of my son so we can get some quality time in." The men chuckled.

Dinner with his dad had been uneventful. Thomas thought he'd brooch the subject of performing a mock surgery to see if the jitters had gone. He decided against it. It was such a good night and he didn't want to ruin it. Thomas wouldn't mind trying again, but only after some more time had passed. He knew it was mental. He just needed to figure out what his brain was worried about and why it started when it did.

His father had his theories, but Thomas had honestly been afraid to face what his father had said. Associating his success rate and patient request added pressure. The pressure of failing. No one had a perfect surgical record, and the thought of losing his first patient under the knife caused his tremors.

There was validity to the theory. In fact, Thomas knew that was the reason the tremors started. It was why he hadn't been to a club in a year. That weight of carrying it all, and his professional career, affected his effectiveness as a Dominant. Thomas wanted a relationship, so when they were at play, he could have the support he needed as a man and a surgeon.

Thomas Valentine's problem? He wanted to be in love.

# Valentine's Day

Brianna woke up excited about today. Even though she wasn't in love or a relationship, didn't matter. She loved the idea of love. Loved love. Single didn't mean you couldn't celebrate a day of the possibility of finding what many people had. Unconditional love.

Brianna got out of bed humming a tune as she showered, dressed and prepared breakfast. Today and tonight would be a great day for her. She would do everything in her power to make sure it was. Answering her ringing phone as she exited her apartment, "Hi Dad!"

"Happy Valentine's Day sweetie!"

Brianna's dad always had the power to lift her even higher. "Thanks daddy. Same to you and I love you."

"I love you too. Any plans for tonight with anyone special?"

Brianna smiled. He was coming from a loving, caring place and she appreciated it.

"Actually, Sunni and I are going out tonight and hopefully Mr. Right will be there. Fingers crossed."

"Sunni! She's a ball of fun so I know it's going to be a great night! Your mom and I are planning a romantic night at home. I'm making her dinner and after, a nice long bubble bath for us."

"Ewe, you could have left the bath out. TMI." The two laughed.

They spoke for a few moments before her dad had to go. Her dad left her in a good mood. Brianna felt her heart blooming a little. So she decided to do something nice.

Brianna had been proud of herself for juggling her bag and the tray that held two cups of Peppermint Mocha. She knocked on the office door and waited.

Professor Valentine's opening of the door took Brianna by surprise, she had been expecting to hear a "come in."

"Oh. I was waiting for you to say come in." He smiled and stepped aside, allowing her to enter.

"I needed to stretch my legs. I've been sitting for a while grading papers."

Turning, Brianna pushed the coffee cup toward him. "It's a Peppermint Mocha and a thank you. For the other day. With Shane."

She bit her lip to prevent the word vomit rising in her throat. Professor Valentine looked good. He had on a pair of dark wash jeans that hugged his lean, firm thighs. A blood red button up that was pushed up his arms, revealing a medical symbol tattoo on his forearm, and a pair of blood red Ferragamo moccasins. Brianna licked her lips as she paused at his midsection. She could only imagine what his penis looked like.

Her head jerked up when she heard him clear his throat.

"How'd you know Peppermint mocha was my favorite drink?"

"I didn't. You always have peppermint on your breath, so I took a shot." She smiled up at him as she sipped her drink to hide the blush that traveled from her neck to her cheeks. Noticing the slight tremor in his hand, her smile slipped, but she adjusted her expression before he noticed. Is that why he was no longer a surgeon?

Thinking back to a conversation she and her dad had at the beginning of the semester. *Brianna's scheduled arrived and she rushed to her dad to get his opinion on each of her professors. Her dad informed her that Professor Valentine was a highly regarded surgeon who unexpectedly quit his career. Her dad also told her his dad was the Chief of Staff and that may have had something to do with his departure.*

"You okay?" He asked, bringing her back to the present.

"Yes. I'm fine. Just thought about something my father said."

Thomas sipped his coffee. "You want to share?"

Brianna definitely didn't want to share. She had questions and wanted answers. However, it'd be totally inappropriate to ask your professor why he left a promising career to teach. It was also inappropriate to kiss your professor, but she did that as well. Not regretting it one bit.

"No, it's not important." Raising her cup. "Well, I guess I should go. I just wanted to say thank you."

When Thomas touched her arm to stop her, Brianna released a shaky breath as her stomach did flips. She turned and looked up at him. He grazed the back of his fingers down her cheek.

"The situation with Shane. Is that something that happens often or?" Brianna tilted her head, savoring his touch.

In a low tone, she responded. "No. I hadn't seen him in over three months." How could she clarify to her professor that Shane was a part of her past? He only appeared when he was stressed. Shane needed someone to dominate to relieve it. It was usually her. Only she was no longer his to control. Losing his touch jolted her from her thoughts.

"He just comes around when he needs someone to comfort him. I'm no longer that person but he can't seem to accept that."

Comfort. The only word Brianna could think of to explain the relationship. Shane introduced her to the lifestyle. She didn't know how to explain what she liked but the more he taught her, the more she realized she naturally fit. He opened up an entirely new world. A world she hadn't explored since but yearned to.

She shook her head. "Sorry, I didn't mean to rattle on. I have to go. Enjoy your coffee and have a great Valentine's Day."

This time, when Brianna walked towards the door, he didn't stop her.

"Thank you again Brianna and likewise. For Valentine's." Thomas raised his cup to her as she exited his office.

· ❤ · ❤ · ❤ · ❤ · ❤ ·

Thomas sipped the coffee as he thought about Brianna, Valentine's Day, and tonight. Using Brianna's words, he needed to find comfort and since he couldn't explore Brianna, he sure hoped her doppelgänger was at the club tonight. It'd been a long time since he played. He wanted a relationship, but having Brianna in his class and the pressure from himself and his dad to give surgery another try had him on edge.

He sent Nick a quick text.

**Valentine:** I hope I find my one on the most romantic night of the year. If not, my little submissive will both regret and love meeting me tonight.

**Nick:** Don't worry, my friend, I believe we both will.

Thomas smiled at the text as he finished his coffee. He aimed the cup to the trash, almost throwing it in. He paused, took a pen and scribbled "Brianna's Dom" and placed the cup in his desk drawer. Grabbing his satchel, Thomas stood, heading to his first class.

The day had been long and full of interruptions. Why did these students believe flower and candy deliveries during class hours were a good idea? His classroom had the smell of roses, chocolates and filled with giggles and sighs. It made his heart swell with longing.

As a surgeon, Thomas didn't have the time or energy to invest in a relationship or be a fully committed Dom. He would never want to enter a relationship with a woman and not be able to fully commit to her or them as a couple. Kimberly was his last serious relationship, she wanted marriage, kids, the entire package. The problem? He didn't love her.

After classes, he met his dad at the hospital and performed a mock surgery. It was successful and gave Thomas hope that one day he could be in the OR again. He understood that if the stress returned, so would the tremors. His dad suggested yoga and acupuncture to assist with the stress. Thomas agreed and explained once the semester ended, he would consider one surgery a month if the relaxation methods worked. Thomas enjoyed teaching but had to admit, he missed the operating room.

On the drive home, he prepared himself mentally for Diamonds and Pearls. He wanted to tap into the Dom persona in advance, since it'd been so long. In his home, Thomas stripped himself of his clothes and entered the bathroom. He looked at himself in the mirror. His body was lean, taut, with brown hairs along his chest down to his penis, which was erect. He followed the trail down, wrapping his hand around it. Jerking off before a night of play was essential to not disappoint the sub.

Thomas squeezed his dick, moving his hand to the mushroom head and massaging it with his fingers. He continued to look at himself as he stroked the tip with his fingers. His brown hair was longer than he usually wore it. As a teacher, he didn't need to keep it as trim when he was completing surgeries. His beard was trimmed close to his face and lined perfectly. His dick became more and more sensitive as he watched himself stroking himself. He closed his eyes as his head fell back.

Thomas slid his hand down his length as he imagined plunging into Brianna's ass. He could see it in front of him, pliable, and warm. He squeezed his dick harder as he imagined how her sphincter would grip him as he pumped in and out of her. Pre-cum seeped from the head. He gathered it, rubbing it over his length while continuing to stroke slow and hard. He imagined his dick easing in and out of her starfish as she sucked him in. He erupted all of his cum onto the mirror. Ropes of sperm also coated his hand as he came down from his orgasm.

Thomas leaned over and placed one hand on the mirror, breathing hard. He opened his eyes and observed the effect Brianna had on him. Labored breathing, a sheen of sweat covering his frame, coated hands and mirror. He smiled. "Miss Bratty Brianna. If I ever get you in my grasp...." He smirked trying to regulate his breathing before stepping into the shower.

Thomas dressed and had a small but heavy meal. He would need his energy, however, didn't want the weight of too much food slowing him. After stepping into his boxer briefs, he dressed in a blood Dolce and Gabbana diamond-jacquard silk shirt, Alexander McQueen cigarette wool dress pants paired with a Valentino Garavani reversible calfskin belt. Red side out. His white Alexander McQueen draped wool white blazer. He looked like sex and smelled like sin. Thomas headed out the door reaching for his keys. He decided to forgo the mask. He wanted his sub to know exactly what she was getting.

Brianna stepped out of the bathtub feeling relaxed about tonight. She moisturized her skin with a glittery body butter and dabbed perfume behind her ears and on her wrist. Her interaction with Professor Valentine had her ready to be thoroughly worked over by a lucky gentleman tonight. No underwear was needed. Brianna dressed in a Michelle Mason halter tie neck backless gown. The gown revealed nothing in the front but the back, revealed the smooth curvature of her back, soft curve of her ass with a bit of the crack peeping out. The silk against her skin had her entire body tingling. It was just the foreplay she needed before a night of sensual debauchery. She slipped into a pair of Judith Liebercrystal Stilettoes, reached for her clutch, the crystal studded mask and her keys, walking out the door.

# Diamonds & Pearls

Brianna and Sunni had to submit test results in advance before receiving the gold embossed red envelope. Even though she was Sunni's plus one, the club's policy was that everyone who wasn't a member have a physical invite. She and Sunni took a car service courtesy of her father. He stated he didn't want his daughter taking an Uber alone on Valentine's. They walked arm in arm to the entrance, which was nestled in an alley with an awning that held a large pearl necklace with tear drop diamonds. All imitation of course, but stunning nonetheless.

"Thank you so much Bri Bri for joining me tonight. I talked big shit, but now that we're here, I'm a little nervous." Sunni squeezed Brianna's arm.

"Don't be. If you become anxious, just take a few cleansing breaths and you'll be fine." Brianna looked Sunni up and down. The gold dress she chose had her dark skin glowing. "You are beautiful and I believe your one is in there." She hugged her friend as she guided her to the door.

Stepping inside, the ceiling was dripping with pearls and teardrop diamonds. They set the lights to a low glow which gave the lure of seduction. The space was massive. The club used off white sectionals as seating throughout, and they had a bar the length of the wall off to the left. Most people were coupled together, however, the single to couple ratio wasn't too drastic. The wristbands they received at the door signaled their status. She played with the pearl beads around her wrist, which meant she was single and searching. Diamond bracelets were worn by the women, who were coupled with men wearing off white silk bands. The men who were available had red silk bands. Brianna surmised it was the crème de la crème of the city. She recognized old money since she was a part of that world.

Sunni walked back from the bar and handed the red drink to her which she accepted. Taking a sip, she hummed. "Hmm, what is it?"

"I don't know. I told the bartender to make it sweet and strong." The women chuckled as they sipped.

Moving deeper into the room, they observed couples touching, fondling and stroking each other. There were no lewd acts in the main area. That was reserved for the rooms, which were down a hall to the right. All the rooms had floor to ceiling glass windows. A passerby could view the activities taking place in the room unless the participants decided to frost the glass. They could see out, but no one would be able to view them.

Sunni paused at a window where a woman was on all fours being face fucked from behind by twins.

"Bri? Do you think they'll let me come in to join?"

Brianna saw her friend's eyes sparkle at the possibility. She looked in and both men were eying Sunni. The woman took noticed as the dick in her mouth slipped out. The woman looked up at the man in front of her, then Sunni, nodding her invitation. Sunni stood straighter and pointed to her chest, to which all three nodded. As she leaned behind her, Brianna stated softly as not to startle her.

"Just remember, if you get nervous, close your eyes and breathe. Let them know this is your first time and if they are good Dom's and subs, they will make sure you're okay." She felt Sunni release a breath. "Have fun and I love you."

She could hear Sunni say I love you too as the door clicked. She turned the knob and entered. While she was happy for her friend, she didn't want to see her in the act. Brianna walked away.

She continued to walk slowly down the hall. As she passed each window, she'd stop, observe each scene for a few moments before moving on to the next. Brianna reached a room where she found two women lying on a circular bed. A red head with her body peppered in freckles, B cup breast and milky white skin. With her, a brown hair beauty with her hair in a twist out. She had light golden skin and a tattoo from her thigh to her ankle. Her breast were slightly bigger, and she had a beautiful round ass.

Brianna sipped her drink and continued to watch as the red head screamed out her pleasure. The brown beauty had her hands on the redhead's inner thighs, keeping them apart as she french kissed her pussy. Brianna's skin heated up as she wrapped an arm around her waist and continued to watch. Once the red head came down, she got on all fours and wiggled her small frame with her ass in the air. The brown beauty stood from the bed, walked over to the wall and reached for a flogger.

She twirled it in her hands, the leather straps fanned out. Once she was beside the redhead, she slapped her ass. It peppered her pale skin with red welts. She slapped it against her ass again in rapid succession, stopping after ten licks. Bending down, she licked each mark before placing her tongue in the red heads pussy, sucking the juices that had trickled down. The process was performed repeatedly. About ten minutes had passed before a man entered the room.

A mask covered his face. His chest was bare and broad, with sleeve tattoos on both arms. He had blonde hair and skin equally as pale as the redhead. The redhead laid on her back, the brown skin beauty got on all fours and placed her face between her legs. The blonde picked up the flogger and grazed it across the beauty's plump ass before slapping it five times in a row. The beauty paused her licking of pussy which earned her another five swats. Blondie placed his face in her pussy and Brianna watch as brown beauty ate red heads pussy while the blonde man ate hers. Just when the two women were on the verge of cumming, the man stood and slammed his thick veiny penis in the brown beauty. He pushed her head deeper in the red heads pussy as he fucked her harder.

Brianna's body was in overdrive as she watched the brown beauty getting fucked hard. She wished it was her. She didn't realize she placed her hand on the glass until she felt a hand cover hers and a body pressed against her from behind.

"I can flog and fuck you better, Ms. Jovi." The low voice said in the shell of her ear.

Thomas and Nicklous walked into Diamonds and Pearls. Both had been nervous. It'd been a long time since either man had enjoyed a place like this. He and Nick had their kinks, but preferred being in a committed relationship with someone who allowed him to play with them only.

"She's here tonight. I can feel her Valentine." Nicklous bounced on the ball of his feet. Thomas smirked at his friend's excitement.

"Come on, let's grab a drink and walk around."

After receiving their drinks, the men walked through the main area. Women noted the red silk bands on their wrist before approaching them. Both he and Nick had women palming their dicks as an invitation for more. While enjoying the attention, the men decline the offers while making their way down the hall to the individual rooms.

As they walked down the hall, the men commented on the couples and acts they were currently engaged in. They both stopped at the same time in front of a window. A light-skinned woman with her hair pulled into a ponytail eased a strap on inside of a man who was leaning on a bench placed at a ninety-degree angle. She had nice size natural breasts with a slight hang to them. Her ass was non-existent. The brown-haired white man was medium build and seemingly salivating, with his dick in his hands, pumping as the woman slowly stroked in his ass until he adjusted to the intrusion. She slapped his hand away from his dick and placed hers around it, stroking with a tight grip as she fucked him harder. He moaned as he began pushing back onto the strap.

The men were turning to leave when they noticed another woman enter. She was black as well. Dark skin with glitter all over her body. She had a figure like the number eight. The men looked and each other, shrugged and turned back to the window. The dark skin woman completed a half cartwheel as the man caught her ankles in his hands. He slowly guided her pussy to his face as his hand firmly gripped her butt cheeks, burying his face into her pussy as she fucked his face by gyrating her body back and forth.

The furrowed brow, lip between her teeth and closed eyes alerted the men the woman with the strap was close to cumming from the stimulation of the strap on. She pumped faster and harder in his ass as she stroked his dick with the same rhythm. She stiffen as she came while jerking his dick. He cried out as he released ropes of sperm onto the other woman's breasts. Once he was done, he continued to eat her pussy as the woman behind him resumed fucking his ass.

"That muthafucker must be high. She was tearing his asshole up." The men chuckled as they moved on.

· ♥ · ♥ · ♥ · ♥ · ♥ ·

"It's her." Nicklous said in a soft voice as his eyes focused on the room they were now standing in front of. There was a beautiful chocolate woman with gold material nestled in the middle of her waist. A man had a hold of her hips as he pounded her from behind. The other man was on his back underneath her, eating her pussy as she inhaled his dick. There was another woman on the bed off to the side of the room, asleep.

Thomas watched his friend watching her, mesmerized. She lifted off the penis as if she knew Nick was watching. She stroked the man's penis while massaging his balls as her fingers pressed beneath them. She kept her eyes on Nick. A smile crossed her face. Chocolate stroked the man harder, pulling his nut from him as he continued to eat her pussy while the other man pounded harder and harder into her. She moaned but never took her eyes off Nick.

Without turning away, Nicklous asked. "Are you going to be okay by yourself? I have to get my future off a of couple of dicks." He rang the bell. The woman removed herself from the men and hit the buzzer. Nick walked in, took her hand, assisted her with placing the dress in its proper position.

"Hi. I'm Sunni."

"I'm Nicklous. Not Nicholas but Nick-lous."

Sunni smiled and pronounced his name just as he'd directed. "Come on. I'll take you home to shower. Also, you're never coming back here. Understood?" Nick raised a brow waiting.

"Understood Nick-lous. I'm assuming I'm..."

Nicklous moved in closer. "Mine."

Thomas smiled, shaking his head as he watched his friend leave.

# Valentine Sex

Thomas continued to peruse the rooms until he saw a woman in the distance. Even with the mask, he'd know that body and those braids with the fly away ringlets anywhere. Her ass was bulging out of the back of the dress. His dick instantly responded.

"Brianna Jovi." He whispered.

Thomas stood there for a moment looking her over as she sipped her drink, completely engage in what was taking place in the room. Thomas noticed from Brianna's body language that she was aroused and struggling to contain herself. The way she sipped her drink. The way she traced her hand down her neck before placing it ever so gently on the glass, swallowing hard. She even twitched at intervals, responding to whatever was being done to whomever was in the room.

Not able to resist, he sauntered up to her. She was so engrossed he'd been able to stand behind her and view what had her so entranced. Thomas blew on her ear to get her attention and placed his hand over the one on the glass. She shivered but didn't turn around.

"I can flog and fuck you better Ms. Jovi." Thomas felt Brianna's breath hitch and the smell emanating from her pores confirmed it was her. Not the expensive ass perfume she was wearing, but her pheromones. It was an earthy sweet scent, and he wanted to lick every inch of her body as he allowed it to seep on his tongue.

On a whisper, she asked. "Professor Valentine? What are you doing here? Did you follow me?" She laughed and shook her head when she realized how ridiculous she sounded.

Before he responded, Thomas untied the mask on her head, replacing it with a black blindfold. She allowed it but couldn't help giving a snarky response.

"How am I going to finish enjoying the view if you've got me blindfolded? Professor Valentine?"

"Valentine. Not the professor. Tonight, I'm going to be your Dom." Brianna took a slow inhale of breath.

"Dom Valentine? I won't be able to finish watching the experience she's having." Her hand reached back as she attempted to grab his penis. He backed away a little.

"I suspected you were a brat the first time we interacted in class. Do you know how long I've wanted to tan that ass of yours for being a bad girl?"

Thomas finished tying the blindfold, grazing his hand gently down her back to the crack of her ass. He moved his hand between the material and her skin in between her ass cheeks. He pushed a finger into her hole. She pushed back. Thomas closed his eyes to steady himself. He didn't want to move too fast, but his little brat was making it difficult. He moved his finger in and out of her at a languid pace, listening to her breathing.

"I want you to consent to everything I'm going to do to your body tonight. He pushed in deeper. She moaned while nodding and continuing to rock back and forth on his finger.

"I also need your safe word." Thomas stopped abruptly and Brianna immediately mourned the loss.

"Red Roses. And I consent to everything you're going to do to my body." She tried to reach back again, but he grabbed her wrist, turning her around to face him.

Wrist behind her back, he pressed his body to hers. Thomas whispered. "I've wanted you since the first day you sat in my class. So be sure you want this because I don't think I'll be able to stop." He cupped her ass. "There will be no going back after tonight."

He kissed her. Brianna pushed her tongue in his mouth and sucked. She took in air when she released him. "Dom Valentine, I want you to do whatever you want, whenever you want, however you want for as long as you want to do it." She placed a kiss on his lips and bit the bottom one before releasing him. "By the way I hate using safe words."

Thomas licked the pain away, tasting the fruity concoction she'd been sipping on. He grabbed her hand and hurriedly walked further down the hall to an open room. Once inside the room, Thomas sat Brianna on the bed that smell of fresh linen. He walked over to the door, inserted his credit card, and the door clicked.

His heart rate picked up at the thought that he'd finally have her, and she'd given him permission to do whatever he wanted. Thomas squeezed his fully erect dick to calm it and himself down. He turned fully, taking in the room. They decorated it in a dark red with white accents. Someone dimmed the lights to almost black. The light bounced off the white sheets, a white chaise that sat in the corner and the white pillows. He watched as Brianna sat on the bed, back erect, hands splayed on her lap, and that damn dress had his Dom rising to the surface. Thomas's muscle memory was back, and he prayed to the Gods she was ready.

When he approached and stood in front of her, Thomas observed her. The pulse point on her neck jumped erratically even though she seemed calm. The rise and fall of her chest and the thin sheen of sweat on her face. She was nervous and excited. "Perfect."

"Dom Valentine? Can I remove the blindfold?" Brianna bit her bottom lip.

"Did I ask you to speak my little brat?" She quieted. Good, she understood play had begun and didn't test him.

Thomas traced a hand down the side of her face to her neck, pressing her pulse. He then moved his hand down to the V of her plump breast which cause an intake of breath from her. "Tonight, I'm going to give you the full experience. Everything I've ever wanted to do to you and more. Some of it will be punishment for past brattiness and the rest..."

He removed the blindfold and stepped away. Walking toward the cuffs that were suspended by chains in the ceiling, Thomas dragged them next to the bed. Brianna's lips were still perched between her teeth. He gently pulled them out.

"Dom Valentine? What am I being punished for? I never did or said anything in defiance." She huffed. Oh, how Thomas hated and loved that huff. That huff was a defiant act, and Brianna knew that.

"For one, that was the second time you've given me that defiant huff. Once in class and now. Second, I asked you to call me Professor Valentine and you stated doctor sounded better and you called me a smart ass." Brianna gasped. She thought she'd whispered it. "And lastly, I ask you not to speak unless you're asked."

He gave her thigh a slap. She jumped. "Stand."

Brianna stood and huffed again as she did so. "My little brat is testing me. It's okay. Twenty licks and I'm sure you'll behave. If not..."

The cuffs were six inches from the bed. Far enough away for him to circle her, but close enough for quick access to it. Thomas raised Brianna's hands up in the air one at a time, securing the cuffs around her wrist. He pushed the chains back, but not with much force. They slid seamlessly along the tracks. Brianna scurried backwards as not to be dragged. He removed the blindfold. The stilettos she wore allowed her to keep her balance. That was about to change.

Thomas placed his hands on Brianna's hips, steadying her. He glided them over her buttocks, down the back of her thighs, legs, and ankles. Once he reached her foot, he removed both shoes and stood. Thomas pushed her stomach softly as she slid back into the cuffs chained to the ceiling. Her feet barely touched the plush carpeting. In fact, she stood on her toes, trying to balance herself. Brianna's hand quickly took hold of the chains above the cuffs that had her wrist secured.

Thomas smiled removing his shirt as he stared at Brianna, who'd paused her movement, fully taking him in. She followed his hands as he unbuckled the belt around his waist. He smirked as his stomach muscles tighten at her facial response. Thomas then removed his loafers, placing them under the bed. He rose to his full height noticing her thighs squeeze and release. His face formed a small smile as he folded the belt, walking behind her. Brianna tried to turn around, but Thomas stilled her with a touch of his hand on her stomach.

"No. Wait for me to grant you permission before moving."
She bit her lip. "Okay."

"Good girl."

He traced his fingers up her back, which caused her to squirm. He moved in closer once he reached the tie at her neck that secured her dress. His lower abdomen pressed against her ass. "I want you to count for me." He whispered to the back of her neck as he pulled the tie. Her dress immediately fell to the floor. Thomas stepped back, raising his belted hand. You could hear the wind the moving belt caused. ***Whack!***

Brianna yelped. She wasn't prepared for the first lick and Thomas didn't give her time to recover. ***Whack! Whack! Whack!***

"Why isn't my brat counting? Do you want me to add more licks for your defiance?"

"Mmmm. Oh, goodness no. Four Dom. Four." She moaned.

***Whack!*** The belt came down one last time as Thomas massaged her bright red ass. Brianna slightly swung back and forth in the cuffs, stretching her toes to the carpet. It didn't halt her movement. He wanted to give her time to come to terms with what was happening, but not enough to recover. Thomas walked quickly to the wall, removing the flogger from the case, he returned to Brianna in record time. Five-figure eights peppered her ass and thighs in rapid succession. She quickly counted.

"One, two, three, four, five. Oh shit!" She whimpered. Thomas was afraid it may have been too much until he noticed the slickness on her inner thigh. He moved up, gliding his hand between her legs until he reached her pussy. He placed two fingers inside of her and pumped. The squishing sound told him she loved it. Brianna's body began moving with his hands, chasing a release. She groaned from the loss when he stepped back. Her head fell to her chest.

"Talk to me Brat. Are you okay?"

Unable to help herself, Brianna responded with snark. "My pussy is wet. I'm horny as fuck. It's been months and you're playing with giving me my dick."

Thomas belted out a laugh as he went back to the cabinet. He responded. "I see I haven't cooled that attitude yet. Maybe this will help." The excitement had been guiding him thus far, but he realized she needed assurance that the pleasure would follow. Thomas tossed the paddle on the bed, spread Brianna's ass cheeks apart and buried his face in her pussy. She tasted like fruit topped with honey. He moved his tongue around and inside her labia, gathering her juices on his tongue. She attempted to push back but stopped when he slapped her thigh with an audible pop and removed his face.

Once she settled again, he continued. He sucked as much of her nectar as he could before swiping his tongue over her bud. She trembled. He latched on and sucked as if he was on a bottle, releasing her after a few minutes. Brianna cried out at the loss. "Brat, you've been a bad girl and Valentine has to correct this behavior so it won't happen again. He reached for the paddle and without warning, swatted her ass five times, throwing the paddle back on the bed once he was done.

"You didn't count which has earned you seven more licks before we're done." Brianna moaned. She was in a sex haze just from the small amount of attention he'd showed her fat cunt.

"Be sure to count Brat because Dom wants to sink this dick in that luscious pussy. He picked up the belt before taking her ankles and placing them on his shoulders. Brianna mouthed thank you from the relief it gave her wrist. Wrapping the belt around his hand, he moved in closer, clasping his mouth over her clit and pussy. He sucked her clit as he licked her pussy simultaneously. She creamed in his mouth which cause him to push his face in tighter to retrieve every drop. Her legs trembled again, which alerted him that her orgasm was on the horizon. Just as she started to stiffen, he removed his face and slapped her clit with the soft end of the belt.

"Brianna?" He warned. "I don't hear counting." He was on the second swat when he heard the numbers around a succession of fucks. He slapped harder as her pussy squirted hot liquid all over his face and chest. Thomas continued the smacks while watching her bud pulse as she started to come down. It was not a reprieve. He latched onto her clit, sucking and licking until she bucked, stiffen and fainted.

When Brianna came to, she was laying in the bed cleaned but still bare. Thomas stood over her. "My little brat was a good girl. You handled yourself beautifully." She smiled up at him.

"Are you ready for me?" Thomas asked as he stroked his engorged penis at her as she nodded.

"Turn your head to the side," Thomas requested as he lit a candle. Brianna complied, opening her mouth, he inserted his dick. She loved the weight of him in her mouth. She sucked his head, moistening it as she slid it further and further down her throat. Once he tapped the back of her throat, she developed a rhythm. Eventually adjusting to the sideways position her neck was in while enjoying the flavor of his dick and pre-cum.

A few moments later, she felt something heating her skin, then tightened it. Opening her eyes, she saw Thomas holding the candle over her as hot wax fell on her breast, chest, stomach and pelvic area. He pushed in and out of her mouth slowly as he continued to burn her skin. She hummed on his dick, increasing the pace the more aroused she became. Thomas sat the candle down and massaged her exposed cheek, "You're sucking so fucking good, brat. Such a good fucking girl."

He moved his hips back and forth, touching her tonsils with his dick. His dick increased in size and redden from the pressure. Brianna prepared herself for the ejaculate she knew would flood her mouth. She was afraid she couldn't catch it all in her current position but didn't want to disappoint him. Thomas surprised her by removing himself from her suction. He tapped her cheek with his dick before leaning down to kiss her lips.

Climbing on top of her, Thomas placed his heavy penis to the entrance of her wet pussy. "Happy Valentine's Day Brat." He pushed in, filling her.

"Happy Valentine's Dom."

# Epilogue

It had been six months since Brianna and Thomas had an explosive night at Diamonds and Pearls. Their sexcapade blossomed into a full-blown relationship shortly after. Both were happy and thriving as a couple.

They were meeting their best friends, Sunni and Nicklous, for lunch. It surprised them both to find out that their friends met that night and had been together ever since. Sunni and Nick moved much faster than they had. They were living together and talking about marriage.

Thomas resigned from the University and had begun performing surgeries once a month at the hospital hoping to return full time. His father couldn't have been happier. Neither of their dads took the news of them dating well at first, but eventually warmed to the idea. It wasn't anything personal, but both men felt it looked bad for a professor in his forties to be involved with his twenty-four-year-old student. They kept their relationship under wraps until the semester was over so it wouldn't adversely affect Brianna's grade or Thomas's standing with the University.

Valentine's Day would always hold a special place in their heart forever.

# Excerpt from Are You Protected

Stephen stood next to his mother's bed. His father looked at her with a tight lip smile and tears shining in his eyes. The smile wasn't returned. Cristina slightly turned away from him. Mickey, whom everyone called Mick, turned to Stephen.

"I'm going to give you and your mom a few minutes."

He released Cristina's hand after giving it a squeeze, which caused her brows to crease into a frown. Mick looked at his son before exiting. Stephen watched the door closed softly before looking down at his mom. Her facial expression had changed. It was a face filled with love. It wasn't as big as her normal smile, but enough to show Stephen she was using all her strength to present her best self.

His mother's frail hand rested on his forearm. Stephen closed his eyes as the tears cascaded down his cheeks as he remembered her healthy and happier. In a voice barely above a whisper, she spoke.

"Stephen."

He opened his tear-filled eyes and faced her. Cristina's eyes were hollow, cheeks sunken and lips cracked even though they were shining with Vaseline. Stephen took a deep inhale, blowing out on a hiccup as the tears continued to fall. His mother lifted a weak hand and wiped his face. She cupped his cheek.

"I want you to promise me one thing?" He nodded, showing he was listening.

"When you finally find your person, do any and everything in your power to hold on to them." She squeezed his cheek as tight as her weak hand would allow. He leaned down, riddled with sobs, and embraced her tight.

"Okay mommie. How will I recognize my person?" Stephen asked in a shaky voice as he pulled away.

"She'll be the opposite of you in every way except one. Just make sure you do everything in your power to protect her mentally, emotionally, and physically."

Stephen looked at his reflection in the mirror. His pale skin had darkened since the weather had changed with a tint of red from crying. His brown hair was long overdue for a trim and his eyes seemed darker than their normal lighter hue. A few freckles dotted his angular nose while bow lips rested below. He whispered to no-one. "The complete opposite, but the same."

His mother nodded at him as he focused back on her. "I'm so sorry I have to leave you honey. I hope you understand someone will always watch over you. I promise."

He wanted to say something, anything to make his mom take back her words, but there were none. When he finally found his voice to respond, the door opened. He moved slightly to go toward his dad as he entered the room. Only it wasn't him.

Instead of his father, it was a tall, brown-skinned man holding the hands of a girl with a perplexed expression on her face. She looked at Stephen, then his mom. With tears now streaming down her cheeks, she gasped, looking from the girl to the man. Her dad. Cristina smiled up at the man and nodded.

"You came?" Cristina seemed to sit up straighter, her face got brighter, and her eyes shone as the man bend down to hug and kiss her on the lips. He gently cleared the tears from her cheeks.

"Of course, I did."

Stephen turned away from the whispered conversation. It seemed they needed privacy, so he focused his attention on the other guest in the room. Her. She seemed to be around his age, thirteen. She had brown skin, like the man he assumed was her dad. A rounded nose and full lips. Her hair had two braids braided along the sides of her head that ended just below her shoulder blade. The girl wore a pink peasant top with dark blue leggings and ballerina flats on her feet.

Not knowing what to do, Stephen looked at his mom, who was staring at the man with love in her eyes. It made him uncomfortable. He didn't understand and why. Their foreheads were touching as they continued to speak in low tones. Both hands were now on the man's neck, stroking him gently.

Stephen moved to the girl when he loss of his mother's touch. A few inches separated them as they gazed at each other momentarily. He reached out and took a braid in his hands. She stiffened a little. He waited until she relaxed before he glided it down to the end of her braid. His facial expression remained neutral as he released it.

"Your hair is nice."

Her expression continued to showcase her confusion, but not fear. She reached over to him, placing her hands on his face. He closed his eyes at their warmth. The girl wiped the tears from his face as she stated, "Thank you. And you're sad. I'm sorry your mom isn't well."

She continued to wipe as more tears trickled down his cheeks. Stephen didn't realize it, but he was mourning his mother's impending death and appreciating the comfort this girl gave him.

With his eyes closed. He leaned deeper into her hand. "What's your name?"

"Charlotte. My daddy said yours is Stephen." He nodded as he opened his eyes. Even at thirteen, she was breathtaking.

Stephen gave a small smile and mumbled. "Charlotte." He would make sure he'd never forget. "Charlotte."

The soft sound of the door opening caused Stephen and Charlotte's head to snap up. Cristina's breath hitched. She was aware the time had come. She saw it in Mick's eyes. It seemed as if time stood still for everyone in the room. Anticipating Mick's next move.

Stephen and Mick stood at his mom's bed as she took her last breath. Before she did, she'd done something that would remain with him forever. She gave his dad a look of contempt before turning to Stephen. Her face softened.

Stephen found it impossible to clarify why, but his heart ached at her words.

"Sweetheart, always remember sacrifices have to be made to save the lives of the ones you love." Christina reach her hands to him, and he leaned in her arms.

"Charlotte's your opposite." She released him and took a few labored breaths.

Stephen found it impossible to clarify why, but his heart ached at her words. "Okay, mommie."

"I want you to remember two things: I love you and always protect the ones you love."

"I love you too mommie and I promise I will."

His father attempted to speak to his mom, but she kept her focus on Stephen as she closed her eyes for the last time.

The hospital, the car journey home, eating, and even dozing off, went by in a blur. Stephen's world had been turned upside down, leaving him numb.

Stephen didn't notice the necklace until the next morning when he removed it from where it'd gotten stuck on his cheek. He assumed his mom gave it to him before she died. Stephen fingered the necklace in his hand as he looked at the charm. It was a silver charm with two zodiac signs on each side. Stephen placed it around his neck.

The funeral was a few days later. Family came, mourned, and offered their condolences. A lot of his aunts offered their numbers if they needed anything. Uncles with promises of future visits to go to games and for ice cream. Stephen just wanted to be left alone. There were also people that he didn't recognize. In suits, but more like security instead of friends. All converged around his dad, speaking in whispers with eyes that constantly scanned the room. Stephen didn't like the chill that moved through his body each time one of them glanced his way.

In his room, Stephen thought of his mom and her. The girl he'd met the day his mom died never left his thoughts. "Charlotte." He had to find her.

"My dad may have been the culprit behind my mother's death, but I will make sure her last request doesn't die with her."

# Rate Your Experience!

**Sign up for my newsletter to stay informed about my upcoming releases and featured Authors!** https://www.darlenecunningham.com

Please take the time to go to Amazon, StoryGraph and Goodreads to rate and/or review my book.

Thank you in advance!

Amazon, StoryGraph & Goodreads

# About The Author

*Darlene Cunningham is an Indie author that writes beautifully flawed characters who challenge the traditional ways of living and loving.*

*She is a graduate of Thee Illustrious Howard University where she completed coursework in Creative Writing, Poetry and Scriptwriting.*

*She currently lives in Atlanta.*

# Coming Soon

*The final book in the Seasons Change series.*

*You know how his life ended. This book will explain how it started. Professor Resto from So This Is College... gets his own story.*

*Camya walked outside the morning after the hail storm. Who knew Atlanta had this type of weather. She walked to her car and immediately noticed the cracked windshield along with the dings along the top and sides of her car. She called Saflite to fix it. Drew arrived and repaired more than her window.*

Made in the USA
Columbia, SC
28 February 2025